James

The 13 Clocks

Adapted for the Stage

by Frank Lowe

SAMUEL FRENCH, INC.
25 WEST 45TH STREET   NEW YORK 10036
7623 SUNSET BOULEVARD   HOLLYWOOD 90046
LONDON   *TORONTO*

SYNOPSIS OF THE PLAY

The 13 Clocks is the adventure of a Prince grown weary of rich attire, banquets, tournaments and the available princesses of his realm, who disguises himself as a ragged minstrel. He travels about the land in his disguise, learning the life of the lowly and possibly slaying a dragon or two, until he hears of the matchless beauty of the Princess Saralinda who is held captive by an evil Duke. The Prince realizes that Saralinda is the maiden he has been seeking and resolves to win her hand in spite of the staggering perils imposed on her suitors by the Duke Of Coffin Castle.

The Golux, who must always be on hand when people are in peril (even though his magic is highly unreliable and his memory capricious at best) arrives to aid the Prince in this dangerous quest.

Eventually, with the aid of a magic rose and a peasant woman who possesses a most extraordinary gift, the Golux and the Prince and Princess emerge victorious over the Duke and escape the even more malevolent and mysterious TODAL.

SYNOPSIS OF SCENES

ACT ONE

Scene 1—Outside the Silver Swan Tavern

Scene 2—Inside the Silver Swan Tavern

Scene 3—A road below Coffin Castle

Scene 4—The Oak Room of Coffin Castle

Scene 5—A dungeon in Coffin Castle

Scene 6—The Oak Room

Scene 7—A road below the castle

ACT TWO

Scene 1—A road below the castle

Scene 2—The forest on Hagga's Hill

Scene 3—Hagga's Hut

Scene 4—Hagga's Hill

Scene 5—The Oak Room of Coffin Castle

Scene 6—A secret passage in the castle

Scene 7—The Oak Room

Scene 8—A road below Coffin Castle

CAST OF CHARACTERS
(In Order of Appearance)

THE WIZARD: The father of the Golux. He lacks the power of concentration which is bad for wizards. Perhaps he finds himself in the Silver Swan Tavern a bit too often.

PRINCE ZORN OF ZORNA: An adventurous lad in his early 20's, full of courage and enthusiasm and devoid of the fear of failure.

TAVERNER: A robust, middle-aged tavern keeper, jovial and prosperous.

TOSSPOT: A young bumpkin who contributes greatly to the joviality and prosperity of the Tavern keeper.

TALE TELLER: The wise and elderly village historian whose wisdom does not embrace accuracy at least when embroidering the evils of the Duke is involved.

TROUBLE MAKER: A grumpy, middle-aged village cynic who is ready to dampen the Prince's enthusiasm with his own persistent pessimism.

TRAVELER: A sophisticated courtier in his early 30's whose manner and dress sets him apart from the villagers in the tavern.

WHISPER: A shadow covered from head to foot in black hooded cape. The Duke's spy in chief. As he is so short lived, this role is usually doubled.

THE GOLUX: A little man of indeterminate age who wears an indescribable hat, a describable beard and a wide eyed astonished look as if everything were happening for the very first time.

CAPTAIN OF THE IRON GUARDS: A brute named Krang, afraid of nothing short of the Todal.

HARK: Another of the Duke's spies in his 50's.

THE DUKE OF COFFIN CASTLE: His monocle gleams in his cold eye. Velvet gloves cover his cold hands. Glittering jewels encircle each of his cold fingers and a necklace of heavy chain rests upon his cold heart. His cane . . . which supports his limp . . . conceals a very cold and sharp sword.

PRINCESS SARALINDA: Moves like the wind in violets, her laughter sparkles on the air and her eyes are candles burning at a shrine.

JACKOLENT: A young dandy whose clothes are in tattered disarray from his hazardous journey to visit Hagga searching for riches.

HAGGA: A simple peasant woman . . . emotionally drained . . . and totally unpredictable.

NOTES TO THE DIRECTOR

After the first production I directed of THE 13 CLOCKS I made several pages of notes to myself for any subsequent productions I might direct. Perhaps some of these notes will prove as useful to you as they have to me.

1. Never lose sight of the story. Keep it moving swiftly towards its conclusion. Beware of lengthy scene changes.

2. A keen sense of adventure . . . urgency . . . and suspense should motivate all characters. Characterizations should not become so intricately developed as to overwhelm the story.

3. Careful ensemble work is essential.

4. Keep it simple. Uncomplicate the scenery and special effects. Your imagination and the audience's imagination should do the majority of the work . . . not special and complex devices.

5. Work out light plan as you go. Have lighting director with you in early rehearsals. Plan one extra rehearsal for lighting and technical effects.

I wish you well.

The 13 Clocks

ACT ONE

At Rise: *The house dims to black, the curtain rises in darkness and lights fade up on a scrim curtain painted in an exact copy of the frontispiece of the book. Directly Center Stage below the scrim line we see the back of the* Wizard, *seated at a table, facing Upstage, wearing antlers. His pointed cap stands on the floor behind him. The* Prince, *dressed as a minstrel, sits facing the* Wizard, *facing the audience and almost completely obscured from their sight.*

Wizard. Once upon a time—wait— (*To* Prince.) What have you done with my hat?

Prince. You weren't wearing one.

Wizard. Of course I was. It's part of the uniform. Officially, . . . as a wizard . . . I cannot give the advice you seek until I am wearing my hat. The sooner you give it back, the sooner you'll hear about the Princess Saralinda.

Prince. Look behind you. (*Picks it up and hands it to* Wizard.) Is this it?

Wizard. It may be. It seems shorter than I remembered it. However, (*Places it on an antler.*) where was I . . . ah yes . . . (*Drinks.*) Once upon a time.

Prince. Must you begin at the beginning?

Wizard. It's usual in stories . . . Of course, if you've something better to do . . .

Prince. I beg your pardon. Please go on.

Wizard. Once upon a time, in a gloomy castle, on a lonely hill, where there were thirteen clocks that wouldn't go, there lived a cold aggressive Duke and his niece, the

Princess Saralinda. They live there still, to this very day and minute, with the thirteen trembling clocks.

PRINCE. Trembling?

WIZARD. Time lies frozen there. It's always then. It's never now. Even the hands on the Duke's watch and the hands of all the thirteen clocks are frozen. They had all frozen at the same time, on a snowy night, seven years before, and after that, it was always ten minutes to five in the castle.

PRINCE. And Saralinda? . . . is she as cold as the duke and his clocks?

WIZARD. The Princess Saralinda is warm in every wind and weather. She is as warm as he is cold. His hands, you know, are as cold as his smile, and almost as cold as his heart. His nights are spent wickedly scheming as he limps and cackles through the cold corridors of the castle planning new impossible feats for the suitors of Saralinda to perform.

PRINCE. Why then, you think . . . it's impossible for me to win her hand?

WIZARD. As a Wizard, who is very wise, I would say . . . in your case, yes.

PRINCE. Why?

WIZARD. Why? You're not a Prince. Oh, you're quite properly a minstrel. A thing of shreds and patches, singing for pennies and the love of singing. That's all very well, but you're not a Prince. And even Princes have tried to win her hand and all have failed . . . I think.

PRINCE. But you're not certain.

WIZARD. I'm not even certain I'm a Wizard.

PRINCE. You resemble one, all except—

WIZARD. . . . Except these? (*Indicates his antlers.*) It's quite all right. I'm not at all sensitive about them. They come and they go. You see, sometimes . . . when I'm bored . . . or in my cups . . . so to speak . . . I cast spells upon myself. They're rather impressive, I think.

PRINCE. I think so too. But if it's all the same to you

I'm not going to give up so easily on the Princess Saralinda.

WIZARD. Ah yes . . . The Princess Saralinda. Well, you mustn't say I didn't warn you. The castle and the Duke grow colder . . . while Saralinda . . . as a Princess will, even in a place where time lies frozen, becomes a little older . . . but only a little older. She is almost twenty-one . . . I think.

PRINCE. I had always thought that Wizards were sure of everything. That's why I asked for your advice.

WIZARD. I am sure of only two things . . . First, you don't seem to be taking my advice and—second—the exact location of an interesting tavern called the Silver Swan. (*Lights up behind scrim. Scrim up.*) As a matter of fact I must take you there some day.

PRINCE. We've been sitting in the Silver Swan all this time.

WIZARD. Then I'm as good as my word. Taverner, some ale here. (*The Silver Swan is filled with patrons who become curious and gradually add their advice to the* WIZARD'S.) I have here a young wag who wishes to wed the Princess Saralinda. (*All laugh.*)

TAVERNER. That's a good one, Rags.

WIZARD. His name is not Rags. It would be something else than it seems. At least, that would be my guess.

TAVERNER. All right, what is it then?

PRINCE. Xingu.

(*The jovial humor of the tavern fades and slowly everyone turns an incredulous silent stare toward the* PRINCE.)

TOSSPOT. What was it he said he's called?

WIZARD. Xingu.

TALE TELLER. Spell it.

PRINCE. I don't understand.

TOSSPOT. Your name, young bumpkin. Spell it.

PRINCE. X—I—N—G—U. Xingu.

Tosspot. That's what I thought. He's off to a bad start already. That in itself is dangerous, don't you think? (*Solemn general agreement.*)

Prince. I thought it was a pretty good name. It's unusual.

Tosspot. But— It begins with an X, don't it? It's common knowledge around here. The Duke only runs his sword through people whose names begin with X.

Prince. I hate to change the subject but you only talk about the Duke. I want to hear about the Princess.

Wizard. Very well, then I'll tell you about her.

Trouble Maker. But the Duke is the one you must outwit. And that cannot be done.

Tale Teller. Suppose he asks you about his limp.

Prince. The Duke limps?

Wizard. I forgot to mention that. It's because his legs are of different lengths.

Prince. Well, that's logical.

Tale Teller. The right one outgrew the left because, when he was young, he had spent his mornings place-kicking pups and punting kittens.

Prince. —punting—kittens?

Trouble Maker. Precisely— Suppose he would ask you, "What is the difference in the length of my legs?" What would you answer?

Prince. Why . . . one is shorter than the other. (*All react disapprovingly.*)

Tale Teller. Then the Duke would run you through with his sword and feed you to the geese.

Prince. What?— What should I have said?

Tale Teller. Why the one is longer than the other . . . of course. Full many a Prince has been run through for naming the wrong difference. Make no mistake.

Tosspot. And then too, there's the matter of his . . . g-l-o-v-e-s.

Taverner. Oh yes . . . those.

Prince. The Duke wears gl . . .

(WIZARD's *hand stops the rest of the word at its origin.
    All close in on* PRINCE.)

WIZARD. He wears them when he is asleep and when
he is awake.

TOSSPOT. Which makes it difficult for him to pick up
pins, or coins, or the kernels of nuts.

TROUBLE MAKER. (*Slowly.*) Or tear the wings from
nightingales.

PRINCE. Can't we talk about the beautiful Princess
Saralinda?

WIZARD. I've been coming to her.

TAVERNER. Only it would be wise to remember not to
mention his g-l-o-v-e-s.

TALE TELLER. Other's have been slain for offenses
equally trivial. Trampling the Duke's camellias, failing
to praise his wines, or gazing too long at his niece.

WIZARD. Those who survived his scorn and sword were
given incredible labors to perform in order to win his
niece's hand, the only warm hand in the castle.

TOSSPOT. They came and tried and failed and disap-
peared and never came again.

TALE TELLER. And some, as I have said, were slain for
using names that start with X, or dropping spoons, or
wearing rings, or speaking disrespectfully of sin.

TOSSPOT. (*Laughs.*) The game's gone far enough.
You've scared Rags half to death. Look at him. How he
could manage to enter the castle at all is a mystery to
me. (*All laugh.*)

. TALE TELLER. If you can slay the thorny Boar of
Borythorn she is yours.

TOSSPOT. But there is no thorny Boar of Borythorn,
which makes it hard. (*All laugh.*)

TRAVELER. What makes it harder is her Uncle's scorn
and sword. He will slit you from your *guggle* to your
zatch.

TOSSPOT. The Duke is seven feet, nine inches tall and

only twenty-eight years old . . . or in his prime. His hand is cold enough to stop a clock. . . .

TAVERNER. . . . and strong enough to choke a bull . . .

TALE TELLER. And swift enough to catch the wind . . .

TOSSPOT. He breaks up minstrels in his soup . . . like crackers.

WIZARD. Our minstrel here will warm the old man's heart with a song . . .

TALE TELLER. He'll dazzle the Duke with jewels.

TOSSPOT. More likely . . . he'll trample the Duke's camellias . . . spill his wine . . . blunt his sword . . . and say his name begins with X and in the end the Duke will say . . . "Take Saralinda, with my blessing, O lordly Prince of Rags and Tags, O rider of the sun!"

PRINCE. You're right— This game's gone far enough. Ride toward the sun yourself my lordly Prince of Tosspots. (*The* PRINCE *tosses the* TOSSPOT, *catches him and drops him in a chair. Pays the* TAVERNER *and leaves the tavern.*)

TRAVELER. I've seen that youth before, but he was neither ragamuffin then, nor minstrel. Now let me see, where was it. (*Exits after* PRINCE.)

TOSSPOT. (*Rubbing his bruises.*) In his soup . . . like crackers.

(*Lights fade on tavern set as scrim falls and* PRINCE *enters below scrim, carrying his lute. A large tree has been placed Down Stage Left near the proscenium arch. In the darkness the* GOLUX *enters and hides behind the tree throughout the ensuing dialogue, until his entrance.*)

PRINCE. (*Enters Downstage Right with his lute and looks behind to see that he is alone.*) They're right. How can I manage to get into the castle. Hmmm . . . Dazzle the Duke with jewels. There's something in that somewhere . . . but what it is and where . . . I cannot think. And even if I could manage to see the Duke— (*Looks toward castle where a tiny light gleams through one of the windows.*) I wonder what I should expect. I wonder if he would order me to cause a fall of purple snow . . . or make a table out of sawdust . . . or merely slit me from my guggle to my zatch and say to Saralinda, "There he lies, your latest fool, a nameless minstrel. I'll have my varlets feed him to the geese." (*Pause.*) I wonder just what my guggle and my zatch are. Aw . . . it's hopeless. I could never invade that castle. A Duke was never known to ask a ragged minstrel to his table . . . or set a task for him to do . . . or let him meet a Princess. I've got to think of some unexpected way. I've got to think of something . . .

(*The first of the group of* TAVERNERS *begin to stroll across the Stage from Right to Left on their way home. They see the* PRINCE.)

TALE TELLER. *Let's have a song, Rags.*

PRINCE. I don't know any songs.

TROUBLE MAKER. What do you make of that . . . a minstrel that don't know any songs?

PRINCE. Well . . . I didn't mean . . .

TOSSPOT. I told you he was a very suspicious minstrel . . .

TRAVELER. If he really is a minstrel . . .

PRINCE. Wait . . . I've a better idea . . . (*Looks toward castle.*) Yes, that's the way . . . I'll tell you a song instead.

TROUBLE MAKER. Impossible . . . One cannot tell a song. Any minstrel should know that.

PRINCE. Not at all. A minstrel is only a thing of songs and poems. Whether he sings a poem or tells you a song the end result is what matters. (*Looks back toward castle.*)

TROUBLE MAKER. Enough of your chatter . . . let's have your poem.

PRINCE.
Hark, hark, the dogs do bark,
But only one in three.
They bark at those in velvet gowns,
They never bark at me.
> (*Two others join the group to listen. The* TALE
> TELLER *laughs.*)

The Duke is fond of velvet gowns,
He'll ask you all to tea,
But I'm in rags, and I'm in tags,
He'll never send for me.

TOSSPOT. He's a bold one, Rags is, makin' a poem about the Duke.

(*All laugh. At this point, from Down Stage Left.* WHIS-PER *cloaked and masked, enters stealthily and sneaks behind the tree to spy.*)

PRINCE.
Hark, hark, the dogs do bark,
The Duke is fond of kittens,
He likes to take their insides out,
And use their fur for mittens.
> (*Everyone stares at him in silent horror.*)

TALE TELLER. I think we'd better go. It's obvious he's gone quite mad.

(*They exit hurriedly except for the* TRAVELER *who has been standing at the rear of the crowd. He stands staring at the* PRINCE. WHISPER *sneaks closer to them during the following dialogue in order to hear.*)

TRAVELER. Young man, I'm sure I've seen you some otherwhere and time . . . I've seen you shining in the lists, or toppling knights in battle, or breaking men in two like crackers. You must be Tristram's son, or Lancelot's or are you Tyne or Tora?

PRINCE. A wandering minstrel, I, a thing of shreds and zatches.

TRAVELER. Even if you were the mighty Zorn of Zorna, you could not escape the fury of the Duke. I'm afraid you've gone too far. He'll slit you from *your guggle to your zatch* . . . from here . . . to here. (*Touches the* MINSTREL'S *throat and stomach.*)

PRINCE. (*Sighs.*) Now, at least I know what to guard. (*With a stealthy flourish,* WHISPER *spins around and slithers off Left.*) Who was that?

TRAVELER. That—was the cold Duke's Spy-In-Chief, a man named Whisper. Tomorrow he will die.

PRINCE. How do you know that?

TRAVELER. He'll die . . . because, to name your sins . . . he'll have to mention . . . mittens. I . . . I leave at once for other lands since I have mentioned mittens. (*Sighs.*) You'll never live to wed his niece. You'll only die to feed his geese. Goodbye, good night, and sorry. (TRAVELER *exits quickly Down Left, leaving the* PRINCE *below the tree.*)

PRINCE. (*Leans against the tree . . . Looks toward the castle . . . Speaks to himself.*)
Hark, hark the dogs do bark,
The Cravens are going to bed.
    (*A deep chime sounds in the distance.*)
Oh some will rise to greet the sun,
But Whisper will be dead.

(*He sighs. A small arm reaches around the tree and taps the* PRINCE *on the shoulder. He spins around to side of tree and sees nothing. Turns and looks around the tree. We see the* GOLUX *is following him. The* PRINCE *turns back as the* GOLUX *speaks to him.*)

GOLUX. If you have nothing better than your rhymes, you are somewhat less than much, and only a little more than anything.

PRINCE. Who are you?

GOLUX. I am the Golux. The only Golux in the world, and not a mere Device.

PRINCE. You resemble one.

GOLUX. I resemble only half the things I say I do. The other half resemble me. I must always be on hand when people are in peril.

PRINCE. Thank you . . . but my peril is my own. (*Starts away.* GOLUX *follows.*)

GOLUX. Half of it is yours . . . the other half is Saralinda's.

PRINCE. I hadn't thought of that.

GOLUX. I didn't think you had.

PRINCE. Very well— Since you must be on hand when people are in peril, I'll place my faith in you . . . and where you lead, I'll follow.

GOLUX. No . . . no. Not so fast. Half the places I have been to, never were. I make things up. Half the things I say are there, cannot be found. When I was young I told a tale of buried gold, and men from leagues around dug in the woods. I dug myself.

PRINCE. You dug? But why?

GOLUX. I thought the tale of treasure might be true.

PRINCE. You said you made it up.

GOLUX. I know I did. However, I didn't know that at the time. I forget things, too.

PRINCE. Somehow, my faith in you seems to be changing into a vague uncertainty.

GOLUX. Now, now you mustn't judge me harshly. I admit I make mistakes, but I am on the side of Good . . . by accident and happen chance. I had high hopes of being evil when I was two, but in my youth I came upon a firefly burning in a spider's web. I saved the victim's life.

PRINCE. The firefly's.

GOLUX. No, no, no . . . the spider's. The blinking arsonist had set the web on fire. (*The* PRINCE'S *uncertainty changes to certainty and he silently begins to slip away from the* GOLUX *when another deep bell is heard in the distance. Immediately tiny lights begin to shine in all the castle windows on the scrim.*) Tsk. Tsk. Tsk. The

Duke has heard your songs. The fat is in the fire . . . the die is cast . . . the jig is up . . . the goose is cooked . . . and the cat, is out, of the bag. (PRINCE *is momentarily thrilled that his plan has worked and that he is to be admitted to the castle.*)

PRINCE. It worked. It worked. At last my hour is struck and I'll see the Princess Saralinda.

GOLUX. Perhaps . . . and then again, perhaps not. Do you hear a faint and distant rasping sound . . .

PRINCE. No . . .

GOLUX. . . . as if a blade of steel were being sharpened on a stone?

PRINCE. Hmmm . . . Now that you mention it . . .

GOLUX. The Duke is preparing to feed you to his geese. Now we must invent a tale to stay his hand.

PRINCE. What manner of tale?

GOLUX. A tale to make the Duke believe that slaying you would light a light in someone else's heart. He hates a light in people's hearts. So you must say . . . a "certain" Prince and Princess can't be wed until the evening of the second day after the Duke has fed you to the geese.

PRINCE. I wish that you would not keep saying that. About these geese . . . ?

GOLUX. Hmmmmyes . . . the tale sounds true and very like a witch's spell. The Duke has awe of Witches' spells. I'm certain he will stay his hand . . . I think. (*The sound of marching feet is heard and grows nearer.*)

PRINCE. On the . . . evening of the second day . . . after the Duke . . . I can't remember . . .

GOLUX. Of course you will . . .

PRINCE. But the Princess Saralinda—how will I get to see the Princess Saralinda . . . ?

GOLUX. Close your eyes.

PRINCE. Now? But they're coming . . .

GOLUX. You want to see her don't you?

PRINCE. More than anything.

GOLUX. Then do as I say. Close your eyes! (PRINCE *closes his eyes.*) There . . . isn't she beautiful?

PRINCE. I can't see a thing.

GOLUX. Of course, you can. Look closely. She floats like clouds when she walks. She wears serenity brightly like the rainbow. It isn't easy to tell her mouth from a rose or her brow from white lilac. Her voice is far away music . . . And her eyes . . .

PRINCE. Her eyes are candles burning on a tranquil night.

(GOLUX *sees the approaching* GUARDS *and quickly exits behind tree. The* GUARDS *enter as the* PRINCE *sighs . . . lost in his reverie.*)

CAPTAIN. Iron Guards halt. One. Two.

PRINCE. You're right. I have seen her. She's the maiden in all my dreams.

CAPTAIN. Nevertheless, you're under arrest. Seize him! (*The* GUARDS *obey.*)

PRINCE. Yes! Quickly. Arrest me . . . but do not take my friend.

CAPTAIN. What friend?

PRINCE. The little . . . he was just . . . here . . . (*The* GUARDS *all laugh.*)

CAPTAIN. Maybe he's seen the Golux. (*All laugh even more.*) QUIET! TENSHUN! For your information . . . there isn't any Golux. I've been to school and I know. Now . . . Dress up that line.

GUARD. (*To* PRINCE.) You heard him . . . Dress it up. (PRINCE *obeys.*)

CAPTAIN. *Castleward . . . HAAARRRRRCH!* (*They exit marching.*)

(*The sound of marching feet fades in the distance. The lights come up behind the scrim and we see the* GUARDS *lounging around the steps of the main door. In front of them stands the* PRINCE, *his hands bound behind him. We are in the Oak Room of the Castle. It is early morning. The scrim rises as* HARK *enters*)

from circular stairway and rushes toward the
GUARDS. *The* DUKE *enters from the circular stair-*
way and limps to the Upstage seat.)

DUKE. I'm sorry to have kept you waiting so long . . .
I was watching my varlets feed Whisper to my geese. Now
let's see . . . where were we. I believe you were planning to tell me some sort of tale. What manner of Prince
. . . and what manner of maiden does he love . . . to
use a word that makes no sense and has no point? . . .

PRINCE. Prince? Why . . . uh . . . The evening . . .
yes . . . the evening of the second day . . . after I am
slain . . . a . . . Noble Prince and . . . a Noble Lady
. . . Once they are wed a million people will be glad.

(*The* DUKE *rises abruptly . . . slowly he reaches for his*
swordcane, staring at the PRINCE. *He limps slowly*
toward the PRINCE *unsheathing his sword as he goes.*
He faces the captive and places the point of the
sword against the PRINCE'S *guggle and zatch.*)

DUKE. Hmmm! Interesting! . . . No . . . no . . .
We shall think of some amusing task for you to do.
(*Limps back to table.*) I do not like your tricks and guile.
I think there is no prince or maiden who would wed if I
should slay you . . . (*Sits at his table.*) but I am neither
sure nor certain. We will think of some amusing task for
you to do.

PRINCE. But I'm not a Prince . . . and only Princes
may perform your task and aspire to Saralinda's hand.

DUKE. Why, then we'll make a Prince of you. The
Prince of Rags and Jingles. (*Claps his gloved hands*
twice.) Take him to his dungeon. Feed him bread without
water and water without bread.

SARALINDA. Wait Uncle! (*Offstage.*) Do not take him
yet.

(SARALINDA *enters from the circular stairway. She pauses*
before reaching the floor level. The DUKE *rises and*
limps toward her.)

DUKE. Saralinda . . . this thing of rags and tags and tatters would play our little game.

SARALINDA. I wish him well. (*The* DUKE *cackles . . . softly . . . so does* HARK . . . *and so do the* GUARDS.)

DUKE. SILENCE! You Prince Rags are gazing too long at my niece . . . (PRINCE *breaks his bonds and rushes toward the* PRINCESS. *The* DUKE *slashes between them with his sword. The* GUARDS *grab the* PRINCE *and hold him.*) TAKE HIM TO THE DUNGEON! You'll find the most amusing bats and spiders there. (*The* GUARDS *lead him toward the door.*)

SARALINDA. I wish him well.

(*Lights fade. Scrim comes down in darkness. We hear the clanking of chains of the heavy door swinging shut. The Stage is in total darkness.*)

GOLUX. Ai-ai-ai. Take care. You're standing on my foot.

PRINCE. What are you doing here?

GOLUX. I forgot something.

PRINCE. What could you have left in this dungeon? (*Slowly faint glow from dungeon grate lends a gloomy illumination to this Scene.*)

GOLUX. Not left something . . . forgot something. There's a difference, you know. I forgot . . . about the task the Duke will set you.

PRINCE. The story I was supposed to tell him was not a success. How did you get in here? Can we leave?

GOLUX. I never know. (*Something luminous whisks across the dungeon floor.*)

PRINCE. I wish I felt a little more secure about you.

GOLUX. HOOOOO . . . strike a light or light a lantern . . . something I have hold of has no head.

PRINCE. Then come over here and tell me this task the Duke will set.

GOLUX. Task?

PRINCE. The task you said you came to tell me.

GOLUX. I did? Oh, yes. My father always lacked the powers of concentration, and that is bad for monks and priests and worse for wizards. Listen.

PRINCE. Wait— Where are you going?

GOLUX. Away from that thing whatever it may be. (*A white something darts into the shadows.*)

PRINCE. Please try to concentrate. The Duke will send for me.

GOLUX. Very well then—to the task. Tell the Duke that you will hunt the Boar, or travel thrice around the moon, or turn November into June. *Implore* him *not* to send you out to find a thousand jewels.

PRINCE. And then?

GOLUX. Why then he'll send you out to find a thousand jewels.

PRINCE. But I am poor! And we have so little time— a thousand—

GOLUX. Oh come, come. That is another problem for another day. Time is for dragon flies and angels . . . the former live too little, the latter live too long.

PRINCE. It will never work.

GOLUX. Well, I may be wrong, but we must risk and try it.

PRINCE. I wish you could be more certain.

GOLUX. So do I! My mother was born, I regret to say, only partly in a caul. I've saved a score of Princes in my time. But I cannot save them all. IIIIIII don't like this place. Something that would have been purple if there had been light to see it by . . . just ran across my feet.

PRINCE. This plan of yours . . . about the jewels. It just might work if only I can persuade the Duke to give me nine and ninety days to find them.

GOLUX. It's a long time to hope for . . . still the longer the labor lasts, the longer lasts his gloating. He loves to gloat . . . I think.

PRINCE. But if this plan fails . . . what then? (*There is a sound of a stone door sliding open.*)

GOLUX. Oh. I have other plans than one. Someone's coming . . . I must go. Be careful what you say and do. (*Exits into shadows and vanishes.*)

PRINCE. When shall I see you again? Golux? How did he get out of here? (*The glimmer of a lantern is seen.*)

SARALINDA. Minstrel? (*She advances from the shadows into the light.*)

PRINCE. It— It can't be. Princess Saralinda?

SARALINDA. Yes. I've come to help you. I was afraid the Golux might have forgotten.

PRINCE. He was here. I am to tell the Duke a tale about a Prince and Princess who cannot be wed until the second day after . . . Oh . . . no that was the other tale. It doesn't matter, it didn't work.

SARALINDA. It almost worked. At least it stayed my uncle's sword.

PRINCE. Now . . . I remember. I'm to implore him not to send me out to find a thousand jewels.

SARALINDA. Oh—yes—jewels, that's excellent. My uncle worships jewels. It sounds very like a possible task. He'll surely send you out to find them.

PRINCE. It was the Golux's idea.

SARALINDA. It sounds much easier than turning water into stone or swimming a lake too wide to swim. Still, you haven't any jewels, have you?

PRINCE. No. Not one.

SARALINDA. Then you'll need something to guide you in your search.

PRINCE. I was depending on the Golux . . . though of course, I never know how far to trust him.

SARALINDA. Neither do I. He's done a lot of good, though it's usually against his better judgment. You know, his mother is a witch, but rather mediocre in her way. When she tries to turn a thing to gold, all she ever gets is clay. When she tries to change her rivals into fish . . . all she ever gets is mermaids.

PRINCE. That is a great pity.

SARALINDA. And his father is a wizard who often casts spells upon himself. His favorite spell is antlers.

PRINCE. Yes . . . I know. We've met. I can only hope the Golux doesn't take after either parent.

SARALINDA. You mustn't worry. I have something the Golux gave me. It will help you in your task.

PRINCE. But Princess Saralinda . . . Why should you want to help me? I'm not a Prince. I'm nothing but a minstrel.

SARALINDA. A minstrel can be a Prince. And certainly a Prince should be something of a minstrel. It is for you, my princely minstrel, that I have waited. (*There is a sound of chains and the heavy door begins to open.*) I must go. I'll see you before the Duke sends for you.

PRINCE. Farewell.

SARALINDA. Farewell. (*She fades into the shadow.*)

(*The door of the dungeon swings open and a column of light sweeps the room finding the* PRINCE *seated on the floor.*)

GUARD. (*Enters the dungeon.*) The Duke commands your presence. (*Stifles a shriek and leaps into safety outside the dungeon.*) What was *that?*

PRINCE. What was what?

GUARD. I know not. I thought I heard the sound of someone laughing.

PRINCE. Ah-ha! The Duke is afraid of laughter?

GUARD. The Duke is not afraid of anything. Not even . . . the . . . the . . . the . . . Todal.

PRINCE. (*Loudly.*) The Todal?

GUARD. Ssshh!! The Todal. (*Swallows and begins to shake.*) The Todal looks like a blob of glup. It makes a sound like rabbits screaming, and smells of old, un-opened rooms. It's waiting for the Duke to fail in some endeavor, such as setting you a task that you can do.

PRINCE. And if he sets me one . . . and I succeed?

GUARD. The Blob will glup him. It's an agent of the devil, sent to punish evil doers for having done less evil than they should. I hate this place . . . come . . . the Duke is waiting.

(*The* PRINCE *rises and exits. Lights dim up on the Oak Room of the Castle. The* DUKE *is seated at the table.* HARK *stands behind his chair. The* PRINCE *has just entered the room followed by the* GUARD.)

DUKE. SO! It seems you want to tell me you would hunt the Boar, or travel thrice around the moon, or turn November into June? (*Laughs.*) Saralinda in November turns November into June. A cow can travel thrice around the moon, and even more. And ANYONE can merely HUNT the Boar. Hmmm. No! I have another plan for you. I thought it up myself last night, while I was killing mice. I'll send you out to find a thousand jewels and bring them back.

PRINCE. I . . . A . . . thousand jewels. A wandering minstrel I . . . a thing of . . .

DUKE. Rubies and sapphires. (*Walks closer to* PRINCE.) For you are Zorn of Zorna, your father's casks and vaults and coffers shine with jewels. In six and sixty days you could sail to Zorna and return. Couldn't you?

PRINCE. No. No!! It always takes my father three and thirty days to make decisions.

DUKE. That . . . my naive Prince . . . is precisely what I wanted to know. Then you would have me give you nine and ninety days.

PRINCE. Well, that would be fair . . . but . . . how did you know what I was going to tell you . . . and how did you know that I am Zorn of Zorna.

DUKE. (*Laughs. Rather . . . cackles.*) I have a spy named Hark . . . (*Indicates* HARK.) who found your princely raiment in your quarters in the town and brought it here . . . with certain signs and seals and signatures, revealing who you are. Go. Put the raiment on. You'll find it in a chamber on whose door a star is turning black. Don it and return. (*Gestures to the stairs. The* PRINCE *goes and begins to mount the stairs. He is halted by the* DUKE'S *speech.*) While he's gone, we'll think of beetles and things like that. (DUKE *limps back to his chair.*)

PRINCE. (*Near head of stairs.*) If you will not give me nine and ninety days, how many will you give me?

DUKE. I'll think of a lovely number. Go on!

(PRINCE *exits at once.* DUKE *laughs.* HARK *joins and* LISTEN *follows suit. The* PRINCE *enters almost at once in a complete change of costume.*)

PRINCE. If you . . . would give me at least . . .

DUKE. WHAT KEPT YOU? I should shorten your time because of your dallying. However, I will try to be fair. Hark, here and Listen . . . there . . . (DUKE *has indicated empty chair.*)

PRINCE. But . . .

DUKE. They are here . . .

PRINCE. But . . . there's no one there.

DUKE. Don't interrupt me! It's very dangerous.

PRINCE. When you pointed to Listen . . . there was no one there.

DUKE. No one there? (*Laughs.*) Listen is invisible. Listen can be heard, but never seen. They are here to mark the measure of your task. I give you . . . nine and ninety . . . hours. *Not* nine and ninety days . . . to find a thousand jewels and bring them here. *AND* . . . when you return . . . the clocks must all be striking five.

PRINCE. The clocks . . . here in the castle. The thirteen clocks?

DUKE. The clocks here in the castle. The thirteen clocks.

PRINCE. But the hands are frozen. The clocks are dead.

DUKE. Precisely. And what is more, which makes your task a charming one, there are no jewels that could be found within the space of nine and ninety hours, except those in my vaults . . . and these. (*Holds up his jeweled gloves.*)

HARK. A pretty task.

LISTEN. Ingenious.

DUKE. I thought you'd like it. Give him his sword, Listen. He'll have need of it. (*The sword . . . which has rested on the table slowly rises and floats across Stage to the* PRINCE *who stares, bewildered at the jiggling weapon.*)

LISTEN. Well . . . take it . . . you haven't got all day.

PRINCE. (*He takes the sword and unsheathes it.*) One thing more. If I should succeed?

DUKE. Saralinda! (SARALINDA *enters from the stairway.*) If you should succeed . . . she is yours.

SARALINDA. I wish him well.

DUKE. I hired a witch to cast a tiny spell upon her. When she is in my presence, all she can say is this . . .

SARALINDA. I wish him well.

DUKE. You like it?

HARK. A clever spell.

LISTEN. An awful spell.

SARALINDA. It doesn't always work.

DUKE. GO! (SARALINDA *exits quickly up the stairs.*)

PRINCE. And if I fail?

DUKE. Yes! That is the stronger possibility. (*Advancing toward the* PRINCE.)

PRINCE. Perhaps.

DUKE. I'll slit you from your guggle to your zatch and feed you to the . . . Todal.

PRINCE. I've heard of it.

DUKE. You've only heard half of it. The other half is worse. It's made of lip.

PRINCE. Lip? (*Pulls his lower lip.*)

DUKE. (*He,* HARK *and* LISTEN *close in.*) Lip. It feels as if it had been dead at least a dozen days, but it moves about like monkeys and like shadows. (PRINCE *removes his sword.* HARK *laughs.*)

HARK. The Todal can't be killed.

DUKE. It gleeps.

PRINCE. What's gleeping? (*Everyone laughs.*)

DUKE. Time is wasting, Prince Zorn. Already you have only eight and ninety hours. However . . . I wish you every strangest kind of luck. (PRINCE *turns to go.*) There is one last word of warning. I would not trust the Golux overfar. He cannot tell what can be from what can't. He seldom knows what should be from what is.

PRINCE. Very well then . . . (*Takes a deep breath.*) When all the clocks are striking five.

(*Exits quickly as the* DUKE, HARK *and* LISTEN *once more succumb to laughter. Scrim falls in the dimout. Thunder is heard. There is a flash of lightning as the* PRINCE *enters below the scrim.* PRINCE *turns up his collar against the wind and rain.* SARALINDA *enters running after him.*)

SARALINDA. Prince Zorn . . .

PRINCE. Saralinda . . .

SARALINDA. I'm afraid even the weather has turned against us.

PRINCE. It isn't the best jewel hunting weather.

SARALINDA. I had to see you before you left . . . I wanted to give you this. (*She gives him a rose.*) It may help you. (*The storm subsides.*)

PRINCE. It has stopped raining.

SARALINDA. I know.

PRINCE. This rose . . . is it a magic rose?

SARALINDA. No. It's just a rose.

PRINCE. It must be magic . . . since you touched it.

SARALINDA. What perfect logic. I wish I'd thought of it.

PRINCE. For the next eight and ninety hours . . . I'll think of nothing but you.

SARALINDA. And . . . where you'll find a thousand

jewels . . . and . . . how you'll start the clocks . . .
and . . .

PRINCE. Saralinda . . . Saralinda . . . I mustn't fail.

(*They walk to each other and embrace in the moonlight.
They kiss. As they part from the kiss the* PRINCE
discovers that the GOLUX *has been enclosed in their
embrace . . . kissing* SARALINDA *as well.*)

GOLUX. I am the Golux. The only Golux in the world.

SARALINDA. I'm so glad you're here. I was afraid you'd
given up. You will help us, won't you?

GOLUX. I wish you well.

SARALINDA. You must be on your way. Remember the
rose my Prince . . . it will guide you. Farewell.

PRINCE. Saralinda . . . (SARALINDA *exits leaving the*
PRINCE *alone with the* GOLUX. *Distant thunder is heard.*)

GOLUX. Now let's think for a moment . . . a thousand
jewels . . .

PRINCE. A thousand . . . indeed. The jewels were your
idea after all. You may not know it . . . but the Duke
thinks you are not so wise as he thinks you think you are.

GOLUX. I think he is not so wise as he thinks I think
he is. I was there . . . I know the terms. I had thought
that only dragonflies and angels think of time . . . never
having been an angel or a dragonfly.

PRINCE. That's very logical.

GOLUX. So is this . . . The Duke is lamer than I am
old, and I am shorter than he is cold, but it comes to you
with some surprise that I am wiser than he is wise.

PRINCE. Oh you are? Are you?

GOLUX. I am also something else. Never trust a spy
you cannot see. You see, I am Listen. (*They laugh.*)

CURTAIN—END OF ACT ONE

ACT TWO

A few distant rumblings of thunder. Several flashes of lightning. Stage is empty. Scrim down. In final flash GOLUX *and* PRINCE *are discovered sitting on apron . . . feet dangling over edge of Stage. They are not happy with one another.*

PRINCE. (*Pause.*) You said that you had other plans than one. I distinctly remember your saying that several times.

GOLUX. (*Pause.*) I don't.

PRINCE. I do.

GOLUX. (*Pause.*) What plans?

PRINCE. You didn't say at the time. (*Pause.*)

GOLUX. I've got it! There was a treasure ship that sunk not more than forty hours away from here. But come to think of it, the Duke ransacked that ship and stole the jewels.

PRINCE. So much for that.

GOLUX. Of course . . . if there were hail . . . and we could stain it with blood, it might turn to rubies.

PRINCE. (*Thunder. Holds out his hand.*) There is no hail.

GOLUX. So much for that.

PRINCE. The task is hard and can't be done.

GOLUX. I can do a number of things that can't be done. I can find a thing I cannot see, and see a thing I cannot find. The first is time and the second is a spot before my eyes. What would you do without me? Say "nothing."

PRINCE. Nothing.

GOLUX. Good. Then you're helpless and I'll help you. I told you I had another plan than one and I just remembered what it is. There is a woman on this Isle who is some eight and eighty years of age, and she is gifted with the strangest gift of all. For when she weeps, what do you think she weeps?

PRINCE. Tears.

GOLUX. Jewels.

PRINCE. I'm sure you're mistaken again. That is too remarkable to be.

GOLUX. I don't see why. Even the lowly oyster makes his pearls without the use of hands . . . or any tools . . . and pearls are jewels. Now the oyster is a blob of glub . . . but a woman is a woman. And this particular woman . . . Hagga by name . . . weeps jewels.

PRINCE. Anything's worth a try. The thought of the Todal brings a small cold feeling to my guggle. Where does this wondrous woman dwell.

GOLUX. Over the mountain, over the stream, by the way of storm and thunder, in a hut so high or deep, I never can remember which, the naked eye can't see it. We must be on our way. It will take us ninety hours, or more or less, to go and come. It's this way . . . (*Starts Off Left. Stops and turns.*) or it's that way . . . (*Starts Off Right.*) Make up my mind.

PRINCE. How can I? I don't know where this Hagga lives. You do.

GOLUX. You have a rose, hold it up. If Saralinda gave you a rose, I'm sure it will guide us honestly. (*The* PRINCE *holds up rose and it falls over to the left.*) Good. It's this way. You see, I was right. (*They exit Left. Pause.* GOLUX *returns. . . . To audience.*) I will tell you the Tale of Hagga. When Hagga was eleven and picking cherries in the woods one day . . . (GOLUX *imitates* HAGGA.) she came upon the good King Gwain of Yarrow with his foot caught in a wolf trap. WIZARD *appears Down Left with foot in imaginary trap.*)

WIZARD. Weep for me, maiden, for I am ludicrous and laughable with my foot caught in this trap. I am no longer ert for I have lost my ertia.

GOLUX. (*As* HAGGA.) I have no time for tears. I know the secret of the trap.

WIZARD. But wait . . . who is there laughing at me? A farmer and his ludicrous wife? Beshrew them both, I'll turn them into grasshoppers, creatures that look as if their feet are caught in traps even though they aren't.

GOLUX. Lo, thy foot is free.

WIZARD. But it is numb. It feels like someone else's foot, not like mine.

GOLUX. I know the secret of that too. (GOLUX *massages his foot.*)

WIZARD. I like this part of the story best of all. Ummm. That's better. Now it begins to feel like mine again. I thank thee for thy kindness fair maid and gratefully give thee this strange and wondrous power. From this time forth thou shalt weep jewels instead of tears. . . . WIZARD *exit.*)

GOLUX. When people learned of the strange gift the King had given Hagga they came from leagues around, by night and day, to make her sad and sorry. Nothing tragic happened but she heard of it and wept. People came with heavy hearts and left with pearls and rubies. Paths were paved with pearls and rivers ran with rubies. The price of stones and pebbles rose and the price of gems declined until, by making Hagga cry, you could be hanged and fined.

WIZARD. (*Appears as the* KING.) The jewels will be melted in a frightful fire. I will make her weep myself one day each year, and thus and hence, the flow of gems will make some sense and have some point and balance. (*Exits.*)

GOLUX. But alas, the maid could weep no more. Damsels killed by dragons left her cold.

WIZARD. (*Appears at* GOLUX's *side.*) And children lost and broken hearts and love denied. She never wept.

GOLUX. She grew to be sixteen and twenty-six and thirty-four and forty-eight and fifty-three. And now she waits at eighty-eight for the Prince of Zorna and me. (GOLUX *and* WIZARD *exit severally.* GOLUX *returns.*) I hope that this is true. I make things up you know. (*Exits again bumping squarely into* PRINCE *who has returned.*)

PRINCE. I know you do. See if you can invent an answer for this. If Hagga weeps no more, why should she weep for you? Why should we even bother to go?

GOLUX. Your point is a considerable one. I feel, however, that she is frail and fragile. I trust that she is sad and sorry. I hope that she is neither dead nor dying. I'll think of something very sad to tell her. Take out your rose, I think we're lost.

PRINCE. (*Holds up the rose.*) I know we're lost and this rose isn't helping. It hasn't moved in an hour. It's gotten so dark I can hardly see it. Anyway, if we go the way it is pointing now we'll become hopelessly entangled in brambles.

GOLUX. The only light in this forest is from the lightning. Hold up the rose so when there's . . . (*Thunder.*) quick . . . (*Lightning. Rose bends.*) This way . . . (*Exit through scrim.*)

(*Light cue.* . . . JACKOLENT, WIZARD *meet the* PRINCE *and* GOLUX *on hill* . . . *behind scrim.*)

JACKOLENT. (*To* WIZARD.) I told my tales to Hagga but Hagga weeps no more. I told her tales of lovers lost at sea and drowned in fountains.

WIZARD. Tsk. Tsk. Tsk . . . Did you try any tales of babies lost in woods or lost on mountains?

JACKOLENT. Yes, I told her tales of Princes fed to geese. I even told her how I lost my youngest niece.

PRINCE. And she didn't even weep at that?

JACKOLENT. She wept not. Do you go to Hagga's hut?

PRINCE. Yes.

GOLUX. He needs a thousand jewels to win the Princess Saralinda.

JACKOLENT. The way is dark. The hut is high. I wish you luck. There is none.

(JACKOLENT *and* WIZARD *exit through scrim into apron area.* JACKOLENT *waves goodbye as the* PRINCE *and*

Golux *climb up into darkness. Thunder and light-*
ning.)

Wizard. They have vanished in the briars. The brambles and thorns grow thick and thicker in that ticking
thicket of bickering crickets.

Jackolent. Farther along and stronger, bong the gongs
of a throng of frogs, green and vivid in their lily pads,
while from the sky comes the crying of flies.

Wizard. And the pilgrims leap over bleating sheep
creeping knee-deep in a sleepy stream, in which swift and
slippery snakes silkily slither and slide whispering sinful
secrets.

(*More thunder and lightning. They vanish. Light*
cue. . . .)

Prince. (*Enter Down Left.*) How many hours are left?
(*They are tired.*)

Golux. If we can make her cry within the hour we'll
barely make it. (*They approach* Hagga's *Cottage. Scrim*
rises.)

Prince. If she is dead there may be strangers there. I
just hope that she is alive and sad.

Golux. I feel that she has died. I feel it in my
stomach. You'd better carry me, I'm weary.

Prince. Ohhh, all right. (*Slowly he carries* Golux.
They arrive at hut. Hagga *sits inside.*)

Golux. Look, there is no light in her window and it is
dark and getting darker.

Prince. And no smoke in her chimney and you are
heavy and getting heavier.

Golux. It's also cold and getting colder. There seems
to be a smell a little like forever in the air . . . but mixed
with something faint and less enduring, possibly the fra-
grance of a flower.

Prince. What worries me most is that spider's web

there on the door that stretches from the hinges to the latch.

GOLUX. The whole thing is beginning to give me a hollow feeling in my zatch. Put me down and knock on the door. (PRINCE *does. No answer.*) Knock again. . . . (*A pause* . . . HAGGA *opens door.*) WEEP FOR US, Hagga, or else the Prince will never wed his Princess.

HAGGA. I have no tears. Once I wept when ships were overdue, or brooks ran dry, or when tangerines were over ripe. I weep no more. I have turned a thousand people gemless from my door. Come in. I weep no more. (*They enter.* HAGGA *sits by a table. An oak chest sits on the floor.*)

GOLUX. I have tales to make a hangman weep, or tales that would disturb a dragon's sleep and even make the Todal sigh.

HAGGA. Once I wept when maids were married underneath the April moon. I weep no more when maids are buried, even in the month of June.

GOLUX. You have the emotions of a fish. (*Sits irritably on floor.*)

HAGGA. I have no tears.

GOLUX. You also have a limited vocabulary. (*He thinks.*) Wait. Have you heard of the toads in the rice that destroyed the poppycockalorum and the cockahoopatrice?

HAGGA. (*Shakes her head.*) I have no tears.

GOLUX. Listen, the Princess Saralinda will never wed this youth until the day he lays a thousand jewels upon a certain table.

HAGGA. I would weep for the Princess Saralinda . . . if I were able.

PRINCE. (*He has spied the chest and lifts its lid with his foot.*) Look . . . Golux . . . Hagga. This chest is filled with jewels. Every kind the Duke demanded.

HAGGA. I know. But they are the jewels of laughter. I woke up fourteen days ago and found them on my bed. I had laughed until I wept at something in my sleep.

(PRINCE *picks up chest and scoops up handful of gems.*)
Put them back. There's something you must know about
the jewels of laughter. They always turn to tears a fortnight after. It's been a fortnight to the day and minute
since I took the pretties to this chest and put them in it.

(PRINCE *pours jewels back into chest as water begins to
pour out bottom of chest. He places chest back on
floor.*)

GOLUX. All right then . . . you must think what it was
you laughed at in your sleep.

HAGGA. But I don't know. It was fully fourteen days
ago.

GOLUX. Think.

PRINCE. Yes, think.

HAGGA. I never can remember dreams.

GOLUX. (*Paces.*) As I remember, the jewels of sorrow
last forever. Such was the gift the good King Gwain gave
you. By the way, what was he doing so far away from
Yarrow?

HAGGA. Hunting. Wolves, I think.

GOLUX. I am a man of logic, in my own way. What
happened on that awful day to make him value sorrow
over and above the gift of laughter? Why have these
jewels turned to tears a couple of weeks after?

HAGGA. Did you hear about the farmer and his wife
who laughed at the King and got turned into grasshoppers?

PRINCE. Yes . . . we certainly did.

GOLUX. (*Apologetically.*) It only took a minute . . .

HAGGA. Well, after the King did that he said to me,
"On second thought, I will amend and modify the gift I
gave you. The jewels of sorrow will last beyond all
measure . . . but may the jewels of laughter give you
little pleasure.

GOLUX. If there's one thing in this world I hate . . .
it is amendments. (*All sit lost in thought.*) WAIT . . .

WAIT . . . I have it. I will make her laugh until she weeps.

HAGGA. I laugh at nothing that has been . . . or is.

GOLUX. Then we'll have to think of things that will be and aren't now, and never were. I'll think of something.
A dehoy who was a terrible hobble,
Cast only stones that were cobble . . .
And bats that were ding,
From a shot that was sling,
But never hit inks that were bobble.
(HAGGA *laughs. But her heart isn't in it. One or two jewels fall onto the floor.* GOLUX *picks up a jewel.*) Oh, dear, she's only weeping semi-precious stones.

There was an old coddle so molly,
He talked in aglot that was polly,
His gaws were so gew,
That his laps became dew,
And he only ate pops that were lolly.
(HAGGA *laughs a bit more. A few more jewels scatter.*)
RHINESTONES! Now she's weeping costume jewelry.

HAGGA. Well, I'm sorry.

PRINCE. Wait, here's a pearl.

GOLUX. No good. The Duke hates pearls. He thinks they're made by fish.

(*Suddenly from her sulking* HAGGA *bursts into violent laughter. Jewels flow from her eyes.*)

PRINCE. What's happened?

GOLUX. I wouldn't know. She's a difficult woman to understand. It might have been the hooting of an owl or the crawling of a snail. Anyway, this time they're real.

PRINCE. (*Scooping up jewels.*) Are you counting them?

GOLUX. (*He inspects jewels as they both hurriedly fill velvet bag and rise to leave.*) I wish that she had laughed at something I had said.

PRINCE. We've at least a thousand jewels, Golux . . . and . . . and very little time.

GOLUX. May God keep you warm in winter and cool in summer. (HAGGA *keeps laughing.*) Farewell.

PRINCE. Farewell . . . And thank you. (*They exit.*)

HAGGA. (*Goes to close door, sees rose on floor.*) A rose. They must have left it for me. How kind. (PRINCE *and* GOLUX *re-enter below scrim as scrim drops.*)

PRINCE. How many hours are left us now?

GOLUX. It's odd. I could have sworn she was dead.

PRINCE. Are you listening to me? I asked how many hours are left us now?

GOLUX. I should say we have only forty left, but it is down hill all the way.

PRINCE. And when and if we do find our way back to the castle, what about the clocks?

GOLUX. That, my Prince, is another problem for another day. Hurry . . . we're behind schedule already.

(*They disappear down the chute into the orchestra pit.* DUKE'S *voice behind scrim.*)

DUKE'S VOICE. How goes the night?

HARK. The moon is down. I have not heard the clocks.

DUKE. You'll not hear them. Give me some light. (HARK *lights torches. Light cue . . . scrim up.*) I slew time in the castle many a cold and snowy year ago.

HARK. Time froze here. Someone left the windows open.

DUKE. Bah! It bled hours and minutes on the floor. I saw it with my eye. (*Suddenly the* DUKE *begins to cackle.*)

HARK. What's so funny?

DUKE. There are no jewels. They'll have to bring me pebbles from the sea or mica from the meadows. (*Roars with laughter.*) How goes the night?

HARK. I have been counting off and on and I should say they have some forty minutes left.

DUKE. They'll never make it. I hope they drowned, or broke their legs or lost their way. (*He is so close to* HARK *their noses almost touch*.) Where . . . were . . . they . . . going?

HARK. I met a Jack-O-Lent some seven hours ago. They passed him on their way Hagga's Hill. Do you remember Hagga? Have you thought of her?

DUKE. Excellent. Their doom is sealed. Hagga weeps no more. Hagga has no tears. She did not even weep when she was told about those little children I locked in my tower.

HARK. I hated that.

DUKE. I liked it. No child can sleep in my camellias. (*Goes to warm hands*.) Where is Listen?

HARK. He followed the Golux and the Prince.

DUKE. I don't trust him. I like a spy I can see. (*Goes to bottom of steps*.) LISTEN! (*Limps to window and looks out*.) LISTEN! (*Limps back to table*.) I'm cold . . .

HARK. You always are.

DUKE. Well, I'm colder. And never tell me what I always am. (*Removes his sword and slices viciously just missing* HARK *on several passes*.) I miss Whisper.

HARK. You fed him to the geese. I remember they seemed to like him.

DUKE. Silence. (*Pause*.) What was that?

HARK. What did it sound like?

DUKE. Like Princes stealing upstairs. He has only one hour left. (*He goes to stairs. Hears nothing. At which he slashes with his sword. Limps back to* HARK.) What does he feel like? Have you felt him?

HARK. You mean Listen? Or the . . .

DUKE. Listen, of course. Who else would I mean?

HARK. He's five feet high. He has a beard and something on his head I can't describe.

DUKE. (*Shrieks*.) That's THE GOLUX! Imbecile . . . you felt the Golux. I hired him as a spy and didn't know it.

HARK. Look . . . on the stairs. (*A ball comes bounc-*

ing down the stairs and bobs along the floor. DUKE *and*
HARK *watch it in horror.*)

DUKE. What insolence is this? What is that thing?

HARK. A ball.

DUKE. I KNOW THAT. But why? What does its
ghastly presence signify?

HARK. It looks like the ball the Golux and those children in the tower used to play with.

DUKE. They're on his side. Their ghosts are on his
side. (*Goes to window and throws the ball away.*)

HARK. He has a lot of friends.

DUKE. Silence! (*A thing that would be a bird if it
had a head or a goat if it had a beard flies through the
room.*) WHAT WAS THAT?

HARK. I don't know what it is, but it's the only one
there ever was.

DUKE. The Golux can't help Zorn with that uncertain
wizardry of his. I'LL THROW THEM UP FOR GRABS
BETWIXT THE TODAL AND THE GEESE! I'll lock
them in the dungeon with the thing that has no head.
YOU HEAR ME?

HARK. YES! But there are rules and rites and rituals,
older than mountain snow or the sound of bells.

DUKE. Go on . . .

HARK. You must let them have their time and turn to
make the castle clocks strike five.

DUKE. The castle clocks were murdered. What else?

HARK. The Prince must have his turn to lay a thousand
jewels on the table.

DUKE. And if he does?

HARK. He wins the hand of the Princess Saralinda.

DUKE. Saralinda. The only warm hand in the castle.
Who loses Saralinda loses fire. I mean the fire of setting
suns, not the cold and cheerless flame of jewels. Her eyes
are candles burning at a shrine. Her feet appear to me as
doves. Her fingers bloom on her breast like flowers.

HARK. This . . . it seems to me . . . is scarcely the
way to speak of one's own niece.

DUKE. She's not my niece. I stole her from the castle

of a King. I still bear the marks on my hand where she bit me as we escaped.

HARK. The Queen bit you? Good, I'm glad.

DUKE. The PRINCESS bit me.

HARK. Who was the King?

DUKE. I never knew. There was no moon nor star. No lights were in the castle.

HARK. Why haven't you married her before? This is your castle.

DUKE. Because her nurse turned out to be a witch who cast a spell on me. I cannot wed her till the day she's twenty-one, and that day is tomorrow. Until then I must keep her in a chamber. Safe from me. I've done that.

HARK. I like that part.

DUKE. I hate it. I must give and grant the right to any Prince to seek her hand in marriage. I've done that, too.

HARK. In spells of this sort one always finds a loophole . . . by means of which the RIGHT Prince can win the hand of the Princess, in spite of the tasks you set him. How did the witch announce that part of it?

DUKE. Like this. "She can be saved . . . and you destroyed . . . only by a Prince whose name begins with X and doesn't." Now we both know there is no Prince whose name begins with X and doesn't.

HARK. No . . . that's not quite true. The Prince is Zorn of Zorna, but to your terror and distaste he once posed as a minstrel. His name was Xingu then . . . and wasn't. This is the PRINCE whose name begins with X and doesn't.

DUKE. (*He is visibly shaken by this fact.*) NOBODY EVER TELLS ME ANYTHING! How much time have they got?

HARK. Half an hour, I think.

DUKE. They're upstairs, I know it. Call out the guards.

HARK. The guards are guarding the clocks. You wanted it that way. There are eleven guards and each one guards a clock. You and I are guarding these.

DUKE. Call out the guards!! Tell them to follow me.

(*Limps to stairs.*) I'll have their guggles on my sword for playing games with me. I'll slay the Golux and the Prince and marry Saralinda myself. (*Exits upstairs.* HARK *makes a face and exits Down Right.*)

HARK. (*In distance.*) Guards! Guards!

(*Stage is deserted. Slowly a light comes up from floor and* GOLUX'S *head appears from trap in floor. He enters . . . followed by* SARALINDA.)

GOLUX. SSSSShhhhh. They've gone.

SARALINDA. But I still don't understand. However did you find the castle without my rose. The Duke would not let me burn a torch in the window for you.

GOLUX. You never listen to me. I told you, you showed us the way.

SARALINDA. But how? I did nothing.

GOLUX. You lighted up your window like a star and we could see the castle from afar. But enough of this, our time is marked in minutes. Quickly, you must start the clocks.

SARALINDA. I? I can't start these clocks. I know nothing about them. Except, of course, that they're dead. (*Sound of furious swordplay comes from upstairs.*)

DUKE. AAAAHHHHH. OVER HERE KRANG. I'VE GOT HIM NOW . . . I think.

SARALINDA. Oh my poor Prince. He faces thirteen men and that is hard.

GOLUX. We face thirteen clocks and that is harder. Come now. Please start the clocks.

SARALINDA. I would love to . . . but how?

GOLUX. Your hand is warmer than the snow is cold . . . touch the first clock with your hand. (*She does. Nothing happens.*) Hmm. Try it again. (*She rubs her hands together to make them warmer and tries again. Still nothing.*) Tsk . . . tsk. Then it's clear to me. We're ruined.

SARALINDA. Now, now . . . you're giving up too easily. Use magic.

GOLUX. I have no magic to depend on.

SARALINDA. Your mother was a witch, your father, a Wizard.

GOLUX. But they never trusted me with spells and things. They didn't want to spoil me. Try the other clock.

SARALINDA. (*She does and nothing happens.*) Then if we can't use magic, try logic. That might work. (*Sword play comes closer.*)

GOLUX. Logic. Now, let me see. I am a man of logic in my way. So . . . if you can touch the clocks and never start them . . . then you can start the clocks and never touch them. That's logic as I know and use it. Hold your hand this far away.

SARALINDA. I hope your logic works.

GOLUX. Now that far.

SARALINDA. I don't think this will work either. We must hurry, Golux.

GOLUX. Patience . . . patience . . . a little closer, please.

SARALINDA. This seems a good deal more like magic to me.

GOLUX. I think you have it . . . there . . . don't move. You see . . . I told you you could start them. (*Slowly the clocks begin to tick.*)

SARALINDA. I did it. I did it. Come on, there are eleven others to start. (*They start to exit—stop and look up.*)

GOLUX. Look. . . . (*Light cue. A giant shadow passes over the Stage.*) Look, there it goes.

SARALINDA. What is it? It looks like a giant vulture.

GOLUX. That was THEN.

SARALINDA. Then?

GOLUX. Yes. Then spread its wings and left the castle, Saralinda. It's NOW . . . now. (*We begin to hear clocks ticking one after another.*)

SARALINDA. Then we've got to hurry. Come on. (*They exit.*)

DUKE. (*Enters at head of stairs.*) STOP . . . I hear the sound of time. Come out, you crooning knave . . . Stand forth Zorn of Zorna.

HARK. (*Enters following* DUKE.) I tell you he's not up there.

DUKE. BAH. They've got him upstairs. Eleven men to one.

HARK. You may have heard of Galahad whose strength was the strength of ten men.

DUKE. Well, that leaves one man to get him. I count on Krang, the strongest guard I have. The finest fencer in the world, save one. An unknown Prince in armour beat him a year ago on an island somewhere . . . but no one else can do it.

HARK. The unknown Prince was Zorn of Zorna.

DUKE. THEN I'LL SLAY HIM MYSELF. I slew time with the bloody hand that now grips your arm and time is far greater than Zorn of Zorna.

HARK. No mortal can murder time. And even if he could there's nothing he could do about the clockwork in a maiden's heart that strikes the hours of love and youth.

DUKE. You sicken me with your chocolate chatter. Your tongue is made of candy. I'll slay this ragged Prince if Krang has missed him. And what's more, if there was a little more light I would show you on my sleeves the old brown stains of bleeding seconds, when I slew time, in these gloomy halls and wiped my bloody blade . . .

HARK. AW SHUT UP. You are the most aggressive villain in the world. I always meant to tell you that. I said it and I'm glad.

DUKE. SILENCE. Where are you going?

HARK. I'm going into the secret passageway that leads to the Oak Room. Come on. (*They exit.*)

DUKE. (*Offstage.*) What happened to the lights?

HARK. (*Offstage.*) Nothing. We're climbing the secret stairway. (*Scrim is up. Oak Room of Castle is empty.*)

DUKE. (*Voice Off.*) OPEN UP . . . It's stifling in here. (*Trap opens. They enter.* DUKE *notices a thousand jewels on table.*) GOOD GLOBS I'M GLEEPED. It's the gems.

GOLUX. (*He appears on corner of table.*) The thousand gems . . . to be exact. (DUKE *starts for* GOLUX, *but is stopped by chimes. All the clocks begin to chime.*)

HARK. (*Chime—beat.*) One.

DUKE. (*Chime—beat.*) Two.

SARALINDA. (*Entering. Chime—beat.*) Three.

PRINCE. (*Entering. Chime—beat.*) Four.

GOLUX. (*Chime.*) FIVE! The task is done. The terms are met.

DUKE. Where are my guards? And where is Krang, the strongest of them all?

PRINCE. I lured them into the tower and locked them in. The one you find tied in knots, is Krang.

DUKE. (*He suspiciously fingers gems.*) They're probably false. They must be colored pebbles.

HARK. (*Inspecting them.*) I'm afraid they're real. The task is done. The terms are met. (HARK *and* GOLUX *shake hands.* DUKE *is seated with jeweler's glass inspecting them.*)

DUKE. Not until I count them. If there be only one that isn't here, I wed the Princess Saralinda on the morrow. (*Begins to count.*)

GOLUX. What a gruesome way to treat one's niece.

DUKE. Twenty-one. Twenty-two . . . She's not my niece. I stole her from a King. We all have flaws, and mine is being wicked.

SARALINDA. Who is my father then?

HARK. I thought the Golux told you, but then he never could remember names.

GOLUX. Especially the names of kings.

HARK. Your father was the good King Gwain of Yarrow.

GOLUX. I did know that once, but I forgot it. (*To* SARALINDA.) Then the gift your father gave to Hagga has operated in the end to make you happy.

SARALINDA. Very happy . . . I think. (*The* PRINCE *kisses her.*)

DUKE. Seven hundred sixty-two . . . That tale is much too tidy for my taste. I hate it.

HARK. (*Removes his mask.*) I like it. May I introduce myself? I am a servant of the good King Gwain of Yarrow.

GOLUX. Now . . . that I didn't know.

PRINCE. But you could have saved the Princess many years ago.

HARK. This part I always hate to tell, but I was under a witch's spell.

GOLUX. I'm getting tired of witches, with all due respect to mother.

DUKE. I can't even trust the spies I can see. (*To* GOLUX.) To say nothing of those I can't see. I have a score yet to settle with you . . . you . . . device. You Platitude.

GOLUX. Keep counting, you gleaming thief.

DUKE. Nine hundred and ninety-eight. (*Picks up last gem.*) NINE HUNDRED AND NINETY-NINE!

HARK. What?

DUKE. Nine hundred and ninety-nine. One stone short of a thousand. That's the last stone and the Princess Saralinda belongs to me. (DUKE *reaches for his sword. A large diamond falls from one of his rings. None see it except the* GOLUX.)

GOLUX. Unfortunately, I just remembered something I had forgotten until now.

HARK. Yes?

GOLUX. As we were rushing down Hagga's Hill, something, a diamond or a ruby, fell and struck my ankle.

HARK. Oh . . . Dear, oh dear.

DUKE. What were you talking about so secretly?

GOLUX. Oh, nothing.

DUKE. Out with it.

GOLUX. We were just wondering what that thing was.

It looks like one of the Prince's jewels that might have
fallen to the floor.

HARK. (*He picks it up.*) Of course . . . that's what it
is. One thousand.

DUKE. One thousand. (*Pause.*) Well . . . what are you
waiting for. DEPART. If you begone forever it will not
be long enough. If you return no more then it will be too
soon. (*All exit.* DUKE *moves to stairs.*) By the way . . .
What kind of Knots?

PRINCE. (*He and* PRINCESS *pause at door.*) What kind
of what?

DUKE. KNOTS! KNOTS! WHAT KIND OF KNOTS
DID YOU tie Krang in?

PRINCE. Turk's Head. I learned them from my sister.

DUKE. Begone! (PRINCE *exits.*) My jewels will last
forever. (DUKE *plays with jewels on table.*) I miss Whisper. Whisper! Whisper! Maybe I should count the gems
again . . . and if . . . and if . . . only one should be
missing. (*Pile of jewels is slowly melting and water
runs off the table.*) What . . . SLISH . . . IS . . .
THIS?????? Nothing but water. Nothing but a pool of
melted gems and jewels leering up at me. AGH! Dis-
gusting. It was the GOLUX. He did it. He did this to
me. If I see him again . . . I'LLLLL . . . (*Light cue
. . . blackout.*) What . . . Light the Torches . . . GIVE
ME SOME LIGHT! (*We can see shadows in the dim
light.*) Something moved. Who is there? The room is colder
than it ever was . . . HARK . . . Where is that Glup
head? What was that? It sounds like rabbits screaming
. . . something is moving in here . . . I can feel it . . .
something that moves like monkeys and like shadows very
well then. COME ON, YOU BLOB OF GLUP! YOU
MAY FRIGHTEN THE OCTOPI TO DEATH, YOU
GIBBOUS SPAWN OF HATE AND THUNDER BUT
NOT THE DUKE OF COFFIN CASTLE. ON GUARD
. . . YOU MUSTY SOFAAAAAA . . .

*(There is an awful shriek. Pause. Scrim down. Light cue.
. . . PRINCE and SARALINDA in kiss in front of
scrim.)*

PRINCE. Shall we stop at Yarrow and see your father?
It's halfway on the journey.

SARALINDA. Oh yes. We must.

GOLUX. Your ship lies in the harbor. It sails at mid-
night when the village clock has dropped the last of his
stony chimes into the night.

HARK. It sails within the hour.

GOLUX. I can't be expected to remember everything.
My father's clocks are always slow.

HARK. A fair wind stands for Yarrow.

GOLUX. He also lacks the power of concentration.

HARK. I hope to see you again . . . and soon.

GOLUX. Keep warm. *(To* SARALINDA.*)* Stay close to
your mate. Remember laughter. You'll need it, even in
the Blessed Isles of ever after. OH . . . and as my wed-
ding present . . . there are two beautiful white horses
waiting for you at the gate. Come now . . . you'll be
late.

PRINCE. *(All look toward gate as* GOLUX *vanishes.)*
But there are no horses in the stable. Where did you find
such beautiful white steeds?

HARK. The Golux has a lot of friends. I expect they
give him horses when he needs them. But on the other
hand he may have made them up. He makes things up,
you know.

PRINCE. I know he does!

SARALINDA. You aren't sailing to Yarrow with us?

HARK. I must stay a fortnight longer, so my witch's
spell runs. It will give me time to tidy up the place a bit
and untie Krang as well.

PRINCE. Where could he have gone. I thought he went
to bring the horses . . . GOLUX . . .

SARALINDA. Oh dear, he's not at the gate either.

HARK. But there are two beautiful white horses waiting to carry you away.

SARALINDA. I wonder where he could have gone?

HARK. Oh, he knows a lot of places.

SARALINDA. I so wanted to say goodbye to him and give him this. But I'm sure you will give it to him for me. (*Gives rose to* HARK.)

HARK. Of course . . . Now you must go. Goodbye.

(*They exit. Scrim rises and pinspot catches* WIZARD *at table with antlers and props.* GOLUX *sits on back of chair.*)

GOLUX. A fair wind stood for Yarrow, all right, and looking out to sea the Princess thought she saw . . . as people often think they do on clear and windless days . . . the distant shining shores of Ever After. Your guess is quite as good as mine . . . there are a lot of things that shine . . . but I have always thought she did . . . and I will always think so . . .

(*Light cue. . . . Scrim . . . down.*)

END OF THE PLAY

PROPERTY PLOT

ACT ONE:

antlers (worn by the Wizard, on Stage at rise)

tankards of ale (all villagers in tavern Scene)

clay pipe (Tale Teller in tavern Scene)

gold coins (Prince, on Stage at rise)

lute (Prince, on Stage at rise; Optional)

chimes (Off Left)

helmets and lances (Iron Guards, Off Left)

rope to bind Prince's hands (Captain of Guards, Off Left)

Swordcane (the Duke, Off Left)

Monocle (the Duke, Off Left)

2 clocks (Oak Room set, floor or elaborate wall clocks with working pendulums, set at ten minutes to five)

monsters (an assortment of improbable things . . . preferably luminous . . . and certainly frightening . . . for the dungeon Scene)

hand lantern (Saralinda, dungeon Scene, Off Left)

sword and scabbard (center table in the Oak Room . . . Scene 2)

   (*Note:* This sword and scabbard must be rigged by thin wire to the flies so that it may travel across Stage from the table to the Prince.)

a rose (Saralinda, Off Left)

   (*Note:* This rose should have a flexible stem so that it may bend easily and point in any direction.)

ACT TWO:

crown (Wizard, Off Right)

chest with jewels (Hagga's hut, on Stage at rise)

   (*Note:* This chest must be rigged so that water may seep from the bottom . . . as the jewels melt)

velvet bag, drawstrings (Prince, Off Right, carries on for Hagga Scene)

jewels (Hagga, concealed in her apron, on Stage at rise of Hagga Scene)

torch (Hark, Off Left)

rubber ball (large rubber ball with gold stars on it, works from Stage Left down circular stairs of Oak Room set)

THE ONLY ONE THERE EVER WAS.
>   (This flies through the Oak Room set from Stage Left to Stage Right. Whatever it is I would rather leave to you.)

1000 jewels (These work from the Center table in the final Oak Room Scene)

rose (Saralinda, Off Right)

COSTUME PLOT

WIZARD:
  long robe covered with magic symbols, tall conical hat

PRINCE:
  (*As Minstrel*) ragged tunic, black ankle length tights, bare-foot
  (*As Prince*) this change must be made with lightning speed; a long, poncho type cloak with purple velvet collar and trim, covered with blue fleur de lis; the cloak should be white; black tights; black velvet pointed slippers

TAVERNER:
  rumpled tunic and baggy tights, very dirty apron

TOSSPOT:
  this village rowdy wears a rumpled smock . . . black tights . . . cloth shoes

TALE TELLER:
  long robe, skull cap

TROUBLE MAKER:
  jacket, hat, black tights

TRAVELER:
  elegantly attired in rich colors, jewels adorn his tunic, wears a long cape

WHISPER:
  long black cloak with hood, black mask

GOLUX:
  floor length robe, an indescribable hat, pointed cloth shoes

CAPTAIN OF IRON GUARDS
IRON GUARDS:
  grey tunics and black tights, cloaks, boots, helmets which cover almost the entire face

HARK:
  wine colored tunic and black tights, long black hooded cloak, small velvet mask

DUKE OF COFFIN CASTLE:

    heavy robe, black hat with black feathers, black velvet gloves, jeweled rings on each finger

PRINCESS SARALINDA:

    floor length brocade gown trimmed in fur, a floor length cape

JACKOLENT:

    rich but ragged tunic, tights

HAGGA:

    simple peasant dress, slip showing, apron, barefoot

ACTS I AND II
COFFIN CASTLE
OAK ROOM SET

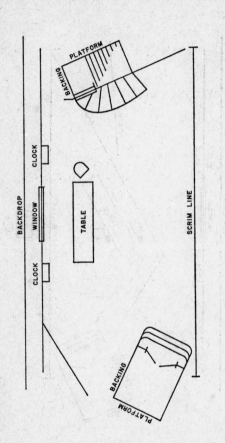

THE 13 CLOCKS

55

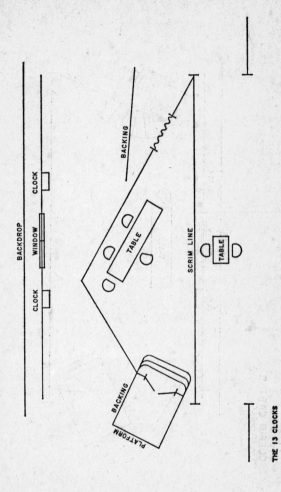

ACT ONE

SILVER SWAN SET

BACKDROP

CLOCK   WINDOW   CLOCK

BACKING

TABLE

SCRIM LINE

TABLE

BACKING

PLATFORM

THE 13 CLOCKS

ACT I
DUNGEON SET

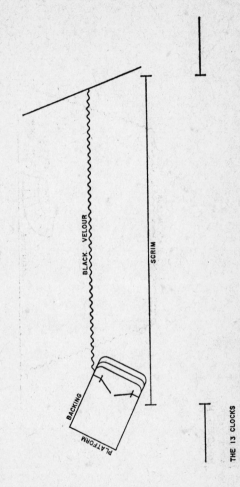

BACKING

PLATFORM

BLACK VELOUR

SCRIM

THE 13 CLOCKS

57

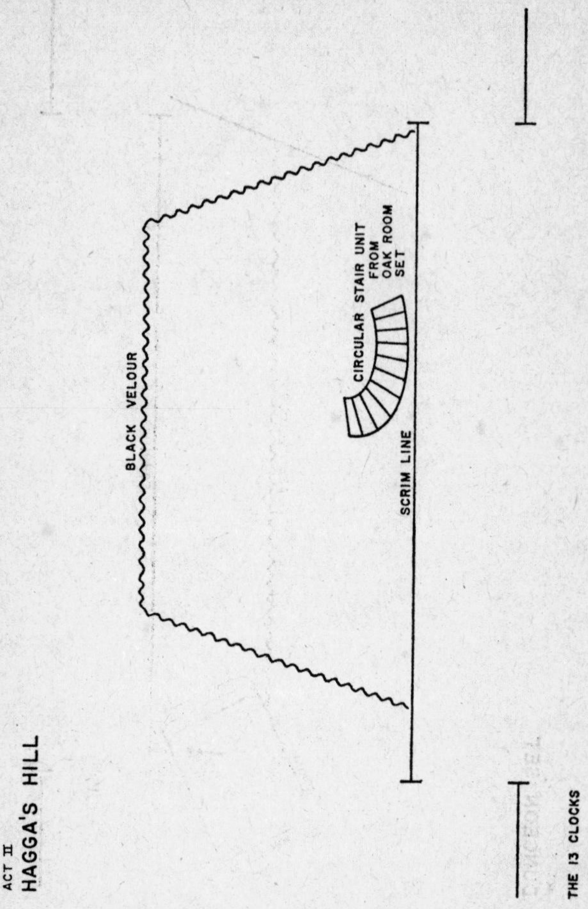

ACT II
HAGGA'S HILL

BLACK VELOUR

CIRCULAR STAIR UNIT
FROM
OAK ROOM
SET

SCRIM LINE

THE 13 CLOCKS

58

ACT II
HAGGA'S HUT

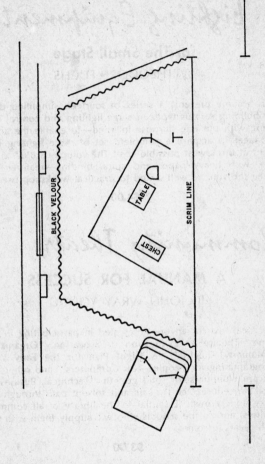

BLACK VELOUR

SCRIM LINE

TABLE

CHEST

THE 13 CLOCKS

59

HANDBOOK

for

THEATRICAL APPRENTICES

By Dorothy Lee Tompkins

Here is a common sense book on theatre, fittingly subtitled, "A Practical Guide in All Phases of Theatre." Miss Tompkins has wisely left art to the artists and written a book which deals only with the practical side of the theatre. All the jobs of the theatre are categorized, from the star to the person who sells soft drinks at intermission. Each job is defined, and its basic responsibilities given in detail. An invaluable manual for every theatre group in explaining to novices the duties of apprenticeship, and in reassessing its own organizational structure and functions.

"If you are an apprentice or are just aspiring in any capacity, then you'll want to read and own Dorothy Lee Tompkins' A HANDBOOK FOR THEATRICAL APPRENTICES. It should be required reading for any drama student anywhere and is a natural for the amateur in any phase of the theatre."—George Freedley, Morning Telegraph.

"It would be helpful if the HANDBOOK FOR THEATRICAL APPRENTICES were in school or theatrical library to be used during each production as a guide to all participants."—Florence E. Hill, Dramatics Magazine.

Price, $2.00

Early Frost

by DOUGLAS PARKHIRST

Drama—1 Act

5 Female—Interior

A tender, yet gripping story of two sisters, Hannah and Louise, who live in a rambling, old house. Hannah has been considered peculiar ever since childhood, when a missing playmate was believed carried off by gypsies. When Alice, the sisters' little niece, comes to live with them, Hannah fearfully insists that she is the missing child returned. While playing in the attic, Alice is visited by a strange illusion, which almost leads her to solve the mystery of fifty years ago. Hannah, fearing her long-guarded secret will be discovered, tries to silence the little girl. It is this tense, cat-and-mouse game between the two that brings the play to a startling climax and affords the actors an opportunity for skillful playing, while holding the audience spellbound.

Price, 75 cents   **(Royalty, $5.00.)**

An Overpraised Season

by RICHARD S. DUNLOP

A Play of Ideas—1 Act

4 male, 2 female—No setting required

A powerful and touching story, "An Overpraised Season" won six out of nine possible awards at the one-act contest in which it premiered. Numerous problems facing today's intelligent and sensitive adolescents are treated in the 40 minute play, which, in episode form, concerns two boys and a girl; a domineering, religiously fanatic mother; and a selfish, egocentric father. A narrator, somewhat like the Stage Manager of "Our Town," expounds the philosophy of the play. A quality play, "Season" is designed for advanced student performers.

Price, 75 cents   **(Royalty, $5.00.)**

The Plotters of Cabbage Patch Corner
Musical Play for Children
DAVID WOOD

6 male, 4 female
Audience participation. One basic setting.

The insects live in a busy world in the garden. Their existence, however, is always overshadowed by the humans—the Big Ones. Infuriated by constant "spraying" the unattractive Slug, Greenfly and Maggot call for rebellion, strikes, ruination of the garden. The others oppose this and war is declared. Fortune swings one way and the other in a series of bitter campaigns. The garden goes to ruin, and the Big Ones decide to build a garage on it. This brings the insects to their senses. They combine to restore the garden to its original beauty and thus preserve their home.

$2.00. Piano vocal score, $5.00. (ROYALTY, $25-$20)

The Ant and the Grasshopper
(Children's Play) Fantasy
ROB DEARBORN

**9 characters (1 clearly female,
the others can be either male or female)**

The classic tale updated with contemporary language and themes understood by today's children—and adults. An uptight, super-industrious ant has just opened a new branch ant-hole when an irresponsible, "hippy-type" grasshopper moves in right next door. Ant resists Grasshopper's offers to join him and his friends, Caterpillar and Ladybug in play—in fact he says play is a bad word. For his diligence Ant is promoted by autocratic, imperious Queen Ant. With his two assistants Ant prepares for the coming winter. Grasshopper, naturally, doesn't believe in winter or any of the gloomy warnings of Ant and even the attacks of hungry Spider fails to daunt his optimism. But winter does come, and both Grasshopper, who has no food or shelter, and Ant, who has no friends and has never had any fun, discover at last that there is more to life than they thought.

$1.75. (ROYALTY, $15)